He's Got to Learn

He's Got to Learn

Alan Wheatley

illustrated by Fabio Nardo

Angus&Robertson
An imprint of HarperCollins*Publishers*

For the kids at Croydon West primary school who like Henry so much and a special 'thank you' to the Croydon Obedience Dog Club - A.W.
To little Sammy – F. N.

Angus&Robertson
An imprint of HarperCollins*Publishers,* Australia

First published in Australia by CollinsAngus&Robertson in 1992
Reprinted in 1992
This edition first published in 1996
by HarperCollins*Publishers* Pty Limited
ACN 009 913 517
A member of the HarperCollins*Publishers* (Australia) Pty Limited Group

HarperCollins*Publishers*
25 Ryde Road, Pymble, Sydney, NSW 2073, Australia
31 View Road, Glenfield, Auckland 10, New Zealand
77-85 Fulham Palace Road, London W6 8JB, United Kingdom
Hazelton Lanes, 55 Avenue Road, Suite 2900, Toronto, Ontario M5R 3L2
and 1995 Markham Road, Scarborough, Ontario M1B 5M8, Canada
10 East 53rd Street, New York NY 10032, USA

National Library of Australia Cataloguing-in-Publication data:

Wheatley, Alan.
   He's got to learn.
   ISBN 0 207 19085 2.
   1. Dogs – Juvenile fiction. I. Title.
A823.3

Printed in Australia by McPherson's Printing Group, Victoria

9 8 7 6 5 4 3 2 1
99 98 97 96

I'm Rosie.
And this is my badly-behaved dog, Henry.

He really is a rascal, but I love him.

Henry digs up plants, tears up clothes and eats them.

He wrecks rooms, chews chairs, chases postmen and terrorises cats!

Mum was always threatening
to get rid of him.

'But Mum, he's got to learn!' I'd plead.

Mum wouldn't listen at first.

But finally it was her idea that we should all take Henry to the Dog Obedience School.

Grandpa thought Mum's idea was terrific.

But when we got there we found out that we couldn't all enrol.

Only one of us could.

It meant spending about an hour every Sunday morning at the school.

Who was it to be?

'I'm far too busy,' Mum said. 'I have to catch up on my paperwork on the weekends.'

Mum's a business-person.

'I have to vacuum the carpets and dust the furniture on Sunday mornings,' Dad said.

Dad goes out to work part-time and does housework as well.

'I don't want to. I just don't want to!'
my little brother Sam said.

So they agreed that since Henry was my
dog, I should enrol.

Funny the way things turn out, isn't it?

Henry didn't come with me the first week.

I had to go alone and listen to a bit of a talk about the training.

'We train you,' the Instructor said.
'You train the dog!'

Anyway, the second week I took Henry along to the Reserve where they did the training.

There were dogs everywhere!

There were big dogs, little dogs, quiet dogs, excited dogs, black dogs, brown dogs, spotted dogs and plain dogs, pedigree dogs and bitser dogs, and they were all attached by leads to their owners.

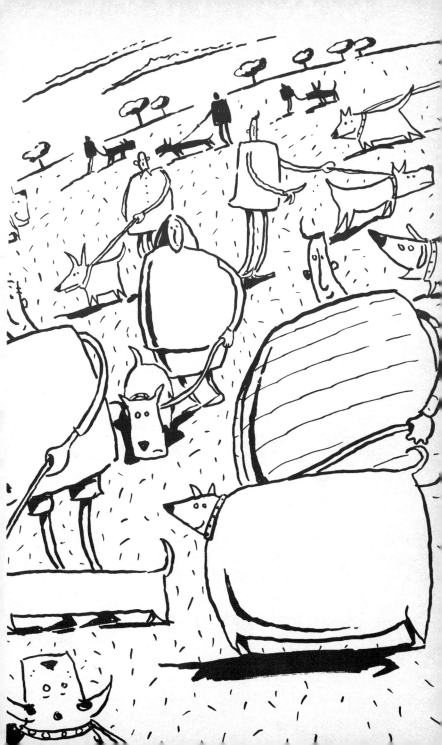

The Instructor at the school
loved Henry on sight.

She picked him up and gave him a big hug.

Later, when Henry found her straw hat
and chewed it up, she changed her mind.

Especially when he swallowed the pink
and red plastic cherries it had on the top.

'I can see we shall have to give you some special attention,' she said in a rather strained voice.

After that, we had some training
in how to sit.

'Sorry'

Actually, we were shown how to train our *dogs* to sit.

It wasn't easy. Henry didn't want to sit.

He wanted to play with all the other dogs.

But our trainer was strict.

'Your dog wants to be the leader of the pack. Make sure he sees you as the leader!'

Henry learned a bit, I suppose.

He learned to sit. Well, sort of. He didn't sit very still. His back part wiggled a bit.

When I got home and tried to tell the folks
all about it, Mum wasn't impressed.

Dad was too busy to notice.

And Sam was in a world of his own.

Sam's a puzzle. Not so long ago he was rapt in Henry. But that's boys for you, I guess.

That night Henry did something unpleasant
under Dad's favourite chair.

Mum of course gave him a good talking to.

I'm sure you've heard all this before,
so I won't bother translating.

'It's no good nagging him, Mum,' I said.

I felt like a bit of an expert in dog-training already.

But Mum took no notice, of course.

I am really conscientious now.

I get up half an hour earlier every morning and practice training with Henry.

We try it with the slip-lead, so he knows who's boss.

I say 'Sit', then 'Heel', and walk quickly so that he will concentrate on what I'm doing and won't be distracted by the other dogs.

Terrific! Yes?

Henry and I make a great team, but no-one
at home seems to have noticed.

Grandpa came round to see how
Henry was getting on.

He understands Henry.

Henry had just been on a rampage around the garden, knocking over some flower pots that Dad had just cleaned.

Then, to top that off, he jumped up at the clothes line and put his muddy paws all over the clean washing.

'You don't make it easy for him, do you?'
Grandpa said. 'You leave everything lying
around and put temptation in his way.'

Henry looked up at Grandpa and a dreamy look came into his eyes.

Grandpa knelt down and put his face close to Henry's.

He whispered something I couldn't hear. Henry sat quietly, his head on one side.

'Honest, Gramps,' I said, 'you're a wonder! How do you do it?'

Grandpa tapped the side of his nose with his forefinger.

'Love and trust', he said. 'You'll find out after a few weeks at the Dog Obedience School. Now I want to go and have a talk to your mother. She's not being very helpful.'

Grandpa's the only one in our family who
Mum seems to really listen to.

Today as you can see,
we're doing a bit of standing.

Henry doesn't like standing.

He'd rather be running, or jumping, or sitting or even lying down. But standing still is definitely not his mug of Milo.

I have to teach him, though.

'It's all part of learning that you're the boss,' our Instructor said. 'And make sure you praise him when he does it properly.'

So I do.

Dad's very good at praising Henry.
The trouble is, that's *all* he does.

'That's no good, Dad,' I said. 'For starters
he can't hear you and secondly he's not
doing anything. So why praise him?'

Dad looked a bit crestfallen.

'You have to be firm with him as well, Dad,'
I said. 'Tell him how much you love him,
but correct him when he misbehaves too.'

I am getting to be very confident about
training Henry.

These Sundays at the Dog Obedience
School have done wonders. I'm not sure
how Henry's going, but I feel great.

I'm not sure that Dad really understands. He's like that, my Dad. Mum reckons he's a bit of a softie.

'It won't help to tell him how good he is,'
Mum grumbled. 'It's plain to see that he's a
thoroughly bad dog. The training hasn't
improved him a bit. If things don't get
better soon . . . '

'HE'LL HAVE TO GO!'
Dad and I said together.

We looked at one another and giggled.
Mum was not amused.

'It's no good laughing about it,' she went
on. 'This is serious. I am not having a dog
in my home who continues to wreck
everything.'

Henry looked quite penitent.

He walked out into the backyard very quietly and lay with his head on his paws, gazing at the magpies chattering on the fence at the end of the garden.

But after a few more weeks at the Dog Obedience School ...

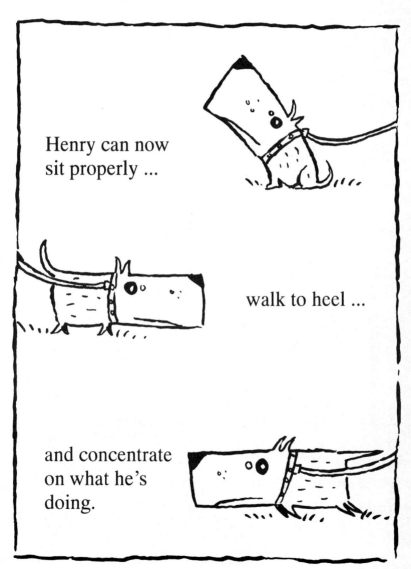

Henry can now sit properly ...

walk to heel ...

and concentrate on what he's doing.

Other dogs don't really bother him. But I can tell that something else is wrong.

If Henry knows that Mum's at home when we get back he doesn't come into the house.

And if she appears at the back door he runs away.

Grandpa came over again. Henry was happy to see him. But as soon as Mum came in, Henry shot off and disappeared.

'What are you doing to that dog?' Grandpa said to Mum. 'I'm beginning to think that you're the problem, not Henry.'

What's upsetting you, Henry?

One morning I was practising with Henry in the backyard.

We were going over 'sit' and 'heel' and then 'stand' and Henry was doing really well.

Then I tried out something we'd done the previous Sunday at the School.

It's really hard.

We had to begin training our dogs to lie down. Or, as our instructor said, to 'drop'.

Henry was sitting down and I had just praised him for that.

I bent down and pressed Henry's back as I said 'drop'.

Henry resisted at first. So I tried again.

I could feel him beginning to go down when suddenly Mum appeared at the back door.

It was the first time she had seen me practising with Henry.

'Is that dog misbehaving again?' she said.

I could feel Henry tremble under my hand.

'Drop,' I said as I pushed his back down.

Henry dropped quietly. I stroked him and made a big fuss.

Mum walked across and looked down at
Henry lying quiet and still.

'I don't believe it,' Mum said in a soft
voice. 'He's actually doing as he's told.'

I looked at Henry and winked.

Well, I think after that Mum seemed to be convinced that his training was working out.

One Sunday she and Dad actually came down to the school and watched me learning how to train Henry.

Well done

'I am really impressed, Rosie,' she said. 'You have both worked really hard.'

And she gave Henry a big pat on the head. Henry didn't know what to do!

Dad began to take an interest in the training too and he came out to practice.

But Sam was off on his skateboard every spare minute he had.

Typical!

On graduation day, Grandpa turned up.
And Mum and Dad too.

We all went through our exercises.

Henry was perfect and was picked out
for special mention.

'This puppy is a good example of how a canine's natural exuberance can be directed into safe, acceptable behaviour,' the Instructor said as she handed me the Certificate.

Then she gave Henry a friendly hug.

Mum and Dad looked so proud. Grandpa looked at Henry.

'I knew you'd do it,' he said.

Then he looked at me.

'Took a lot of trouble with that dog, didn't you, Rosie? Not like some people I could name.'

Grandpa turned to look at Mum.

'Henry will never be a really happy, contented dog until he feels secure and trusts the family,' he said. 'Now it's your turn for a bit of training.'